Sofia and th

Written by Sarah Wilson, PNP

Illustrated by QBN Studios

Printed in the United States of America

ISBN 978-1-7375478-0-8

Illustrated by QBN Studios
www.sofiaandtheshot.com

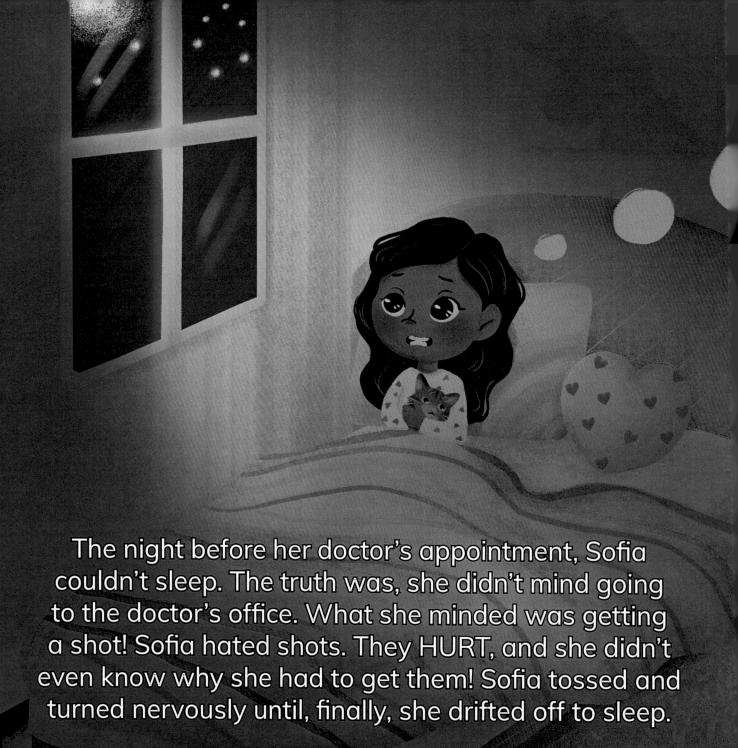

The night before her doctor's appointment, Sofia couldn't sleep. The truth was, she didn't mind going to the doctor's office. What she minded was getting a shot! Sofia hated shots. They HURT, and she didn't even know why she had to get them! Sofia tossed and turned nervously until, finally, she drifted off to sleep.

The next morning, Sofia waited patiently for her appointment. "Come with me, Sofia," the nurse called at last. "It's time to get your shot!" At the word shot, Sofia panicked. Slowly backing away, she turned and bolted out the door.

The next thing she knew, Sofia crashed to a halt, one foot balancing over water. How had she gotten on a boat? Behind her, a voice called out. "Do be careful, my girl. You almost ran right off the deck."

Sofia frantically whipped her head around.
"Wh-who said that?" she asked.

"Why, I did," said a gray cat sitting on the other side of the boat. "Good day. My name is Mr. Whiskers. And what might your name be?"
Sofia stared, wide-eyed and open-mouthed.

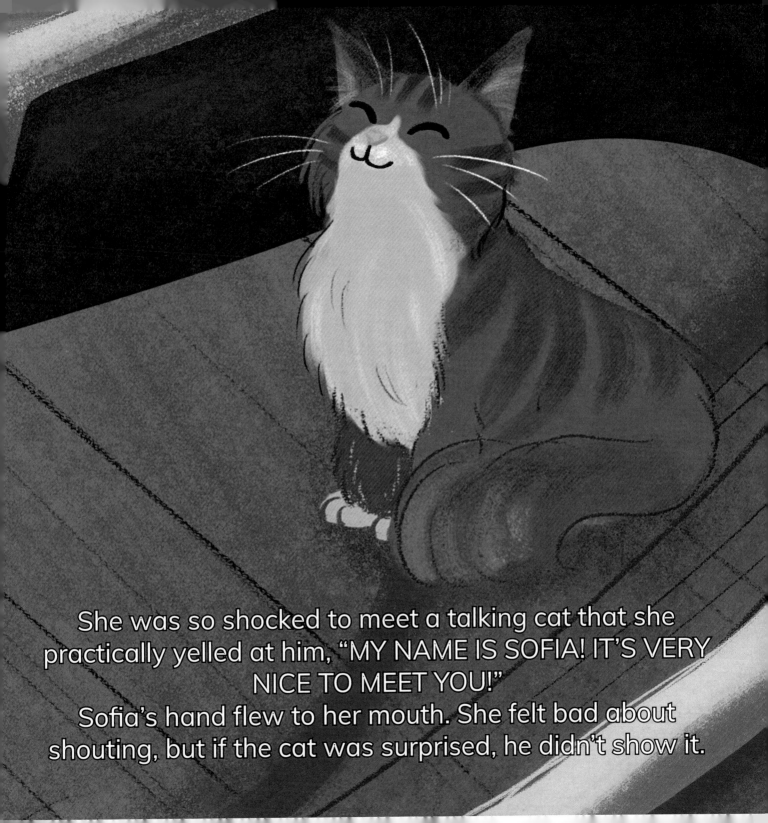

She was so shocked to meet a talking cat that she practically yelled at him, "MY NAME IS SOFIA! IT'S VERY NICE TO MEET YOU!"

Sofia's hand flew to her mouth. She felt bad about shouting, but if the cat was surprised, he didn't show it.

"Lovely to meet you Sofia, may I ask what brings you to my boat?"
"Well, I don't actually know," she replied. "I was at the doctor's office for my appointment, but when the nurse tried to give me a shot I ran away. The next thing I knew, I was here!"

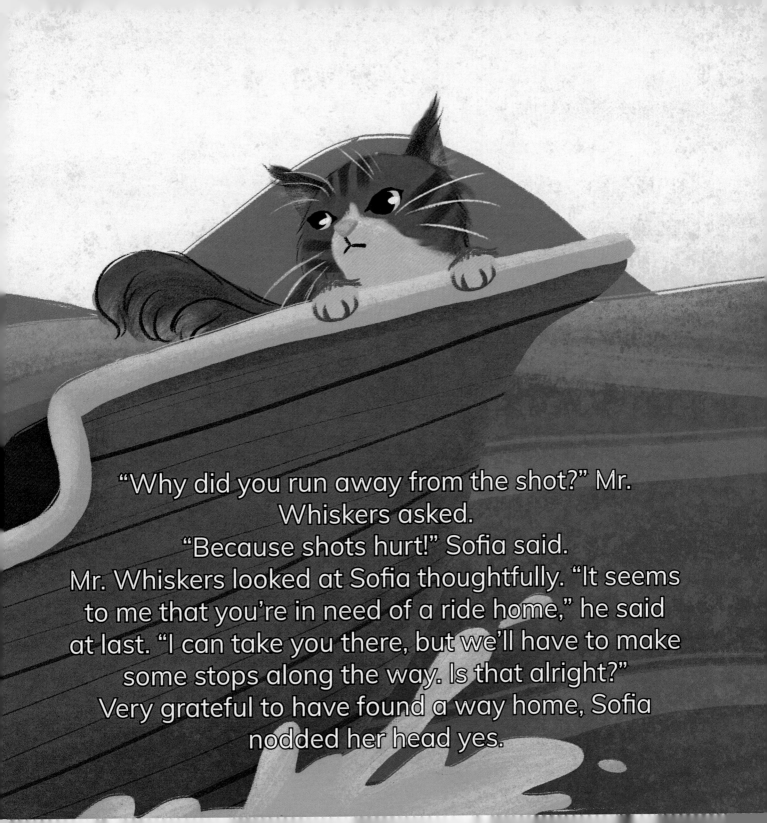

"Why did you run away from the shot?" Mr. Whiskers asked.

"Because shots hurt!" Sofia said.

Mr. Whiskers looked at Sofia thoughtfully. "It seems to me that you're in need of a ride home," he said at last. "I can take you there, but we'll have to make some stops along the way. Is that alright?"

Very grateful to have found a way home, Sofia nodded her head yes.

It wasn't long before Sofia spotted a small
island in the distance.
"Our first stop," the cat announced.
On the shore, Sofia noticed a tortoise.

"Good morning, Mr. Whiskers," the tortoise greeted them. "What can I do for you today?" Instead of answering, Mr. Whiskers turned to Sofia. "This is my oldest friend, Mr. Shell," he explained. "He is 200 years old and was born before shots existed!" "Wow, I wish I had been born before shots!" Sofia exclaimed.

"Before shots?" Mr. Shell exclaimed. "Oh, no! Back then, there was no medicine to protect people from getting sick. Germs were everywhere, and people got horrible diseases. You are quite lucky to live in the age of shots. Did you know, shots have a medicine in them called a vaccine? Vaccines protect people from some of the worst germs out there."

"So, shots keep us from getting sick?" Sofia asked.
"That's right! How do you think I lived to
be 200!" the tortoise replied with a wink.
Sofia thanked Mr. Shell, and the boat
went on its way.

Soon, they came to another island. On the shore,
Sofia could see a herd of sheep standing together.
"Why do the sheep stay together in a group, even if
there is no fence?" she asked aloud.

Mr. Whiskers looked at Sofia. "The sheep on this island live together so that the older and weaker ones are protected by the younger, healthier, sheep. Vaccines are the same. Some people are too young or too old to be protected by them. When a healthy person gets a vaccine, they protect everyone around them from the spread of germs."

"You mean, if I get my shot, I'm protecting others from getting sick?" Sofia asked.
"That's right," said Mr. Whiskers.

As they left the island behind, Sofia thought about her baby sister, who was too young to get shots. She thought about her grandparents, who got sick so easily. She'd never want to do anything to hurt them.

If getting a shot was what it took to keep them safe,
then she'd just have to do it.

Soon, the boat reached its final stop.
"Tell me, Sofia," Mr. Whiskers said. "The next time a nurse tries to give you a shot, will you still run away?"
Sofia shook her head. "I'm glad I know why we get shots, but I'm still afraid because I know it will hurt."
Mr. Whiskers looked at her thoughtfully. "A shot only hurts for a minute, but the germs that shots protect us against can make us feel terrible for days. Sometimes they make us so sick that we don't get better."

Sofia thought about how awful she'd felt the last time she was sick. "You're right, getting a shot is a lot better than getting sick. When I go back to the doctor, I'm going to be brave."

"My dear girl, I think that is a very wise decision," Mr. Whiskers said. "You are very brave, indeed."

Suddenly, Sofia heard a voice calling her name.
"It was nice to meet you, Mr. Whiskers," she said.
"Thank you for teaching me about shots!"
"It was my pleasure," he replied. "But now I think
it's time for you to wake up."
Confused, Sofia looked at her new friend.
"But I am awake."

The voice called softly again, and Mr. Whiskers
faded from view.
Opening her eyes, Sofia saw her mom looking
at her from the door of her bedroom.

"Come on, Sofia. We don't want to be late for your appointment."

That day at the doctor's office, Sofia was very brave as she got her shot. "That wasn't so bad," she said afterward. Her mom looked at her with wonder in her eyes and said, "Sofia, you're the bravest girl I've ever met."

And the two walked out of the office and headed home.

Sarah Wilson is a Pediatric Nurse Practitioner based in Broomfield, CO. After seeing the magic of children's books prepare her patients for a check up, she created *Sofia and the Shot* in order to help young children understand the importance of vaccines. When she is not working or writing children's books, Sarah enjoys traveling, baking, and spending time with her family and two cats.

Made in United States
North Haven, CT
15 June 2022

20285916R00022